The Changeling

The Changeling

By Terri Windling

BULLSEYE CHILLERS™

RANDOM HOUSE 🏠 **NEW YORK**

Dedicated to the lads:

Robin Sickafoose, Toby Froud,
Ben Lewis, and Eddy Martinez

A BULLSEYE BOOK PUBLISHED BY RANDOM HOUSE, INC.

Text copyright © 1995 by Terri Windling
Cover illustration copyright © 1995 by Jim Warren
All rights reserved under International and Pan-American Copyright Conventions.
Published in the United States by Random House, Inc., New York, and
simultaneously in Canada by Random House of Canada Limited, Toronto.

Library of Congress Cataloging-in-Publication Data
Windling, Terri.
    The changeling / by Terri Windling.
       p. cm. — (Bullseye chillers)
    SUMMARY: Twelve-year-old Charlie must fiddle all night to save his sister who
has been kidnapped by faeries.
    ISBN 0-679-86699-X (pbk.)
    [1. Fairies—Fiction. 2. Fiddling—Fiction. 3. Brothers and sisters—Fiction.]
I. Title. II. Series.
    PZ7.W72437Ch 1995 [Fic]—dc20 94-32010

Manufactured in the United States of America 10 9 8 7 6 5 4 3 2 1

Contents

CHAPTER ONE

DEATH AND THE FIDDLE MAN

There was no music on the afternoon my father's coffin was lowered into the ground. There should have been. My father loved music more than anything in the world. Maybe even more than his family. That's what the neighbors said, anyway, even when he was alive. First they said it behind my mother's back. Then they said it right out in the open, when my mother had to go and find a job even though she had a baby at home.

It wasn't that my pa didn't want to work. It was just that music was the only work he knew. He'd been a fiddle man all his life. He played the fiddle at weddings and dances all over North Carolina. Used to be he'd earn a good living at it, too.

Until the week the twins died. One after the other. And then all the joy went out of his music. No one would hire him to play. Folks said his fiddle was haunted. All it would play was his sorrow.

It was just last spring, about this time, that we lost my brother Billy. He was a tall, strong boy. Sixteen years old and always laughing, that's what I remember. And then suddenly my brother was dead. And I was standing next to Pa while Billy's coffin was lowered into the red Carolina clay.

Just one week later we lost the other

twin, Jimmy Jr. We buried him at Billy's side. Pa played the funeral march. The fiddle made a low and lonesome sound. Tears were running down Pa's face. Mama stood stiff and quiet.

My brothers had died of consumption. That's what we called tuberculosis. It was a sickness we all feared in those days. The doctors didn't have any medicine for it. We could only look on helplessly as the twins grew thin and pale as ghosts. As they coughed blood and then died.

When Pa grew pale, I prayed it was from grief. Death had stolen so much from my family already. He'd stolen Billy and Jimmy both. And Pa's music. And my mother's smile. How could he ask any more of us? Then Pa began to cough up blood. The night Death came knocking on our door again, Pa called me to his bedside.

"Charlie," he said. His voice was a whisper. "I know you are only twelve years old. But you are the man of the family now. You take good care of your mama. You look after your sister Polly. And don't you ever let go of the music, like I did. Promise me, boy." He reached for my hand.

I sat beside my daddy's bed. I held his cold, white hand in mine. I promised him I would never let go. He smiled and closed his eyes. When Mama came up with his supper on a tray, my pa was already gone.

After the funeral, we came back to a dark and empty house. It used to be that we had boarders. The boarders were young men who lived with us while they went to school at a college nearby. Mama cooked their meals and washed their clothes. It earned us a little extra money.

But the boarders left, one by one, when Pa got sick like my brothers. Everyone was scared they'd catch consumption in our house. They said my family was contagious.

I knew my mama was worried about how to make ends meet with the boarders gone. She was the town's best schoolteacher—everybody said so. But in those days a schoolteacher's pay wasn't enough to raise a family on.

Mama didn't speak about her worries to me. She told me and Polly that we would be just fine. She said that Pa would watch over us from heaven. But Mama had that pinched look on her face that she got when she was scared.

We ate a simple supper together. It felt strange that there were just three of us left around the big kitchen table. Everything was different now. Mama had not been to work since Pa died. I had not been to school.

There were so many questions I wanted to ask. Would Old Lady Grundy still come take care of Polly when Mama went back to teach school? Would I still be going to school myself? Or would I have to quit school and work, now that I was the man of the house?

I had always wanted to grow up to be a fiddle man, just like my pa. I practiced hard. And I was good. But who was going to hire a mere boy to play when they wouldn't even hire my daddy?

I wanted to ask Mama all these things. But the words stuck like a lump in my throat. Mama was silent. She barely touched her food. Even three-year-old Polly was quiet.

By the time the supper dishes were washed and dried, I couldn't stand the

silence anymore. Back before the twins had died, I'd never heard silence in this house. Not unless we were all fast asleep.

I remembered my brothers laughing, the baby crying for her bottle, the boarders arguing over politics. I remembered Pa's fiddle and the instruments of his musician friends filling up the house with music at all hours of the day.

I followed my mother into the parlor. She lit the oil lamp. Then she sat down with her sewing basket, just like she did every night. Little Polly snuggled beside her, her thumb in her mouth, her eyes heavy with sleep. Mama just sat there with her needle and thread, like she couldn't remember what to do with them.

I thought about my promise to Pa. I took my fiddle down from its hook on the wall. My daddy's fiddle hung beside it, dusty and neglected. It was my fiddle

now, but I was scared to play it. What if it really was haunted? What if it held all Pa's sorrow in the hollow in the middle? I had enough sorrow of my own.

I tuned my own fiddle and tightened the bow. I ran rosin across its horsehair strands. Then I tucked the fiddle beneath my chin and ran the bow across the strings.

I played "O'Carolan's Farewell." It was an Irish tune that my daddy loved. The music was low and sweet and sad. I saw tears run down my mother's face. I'd never seen her cry before. She was always brave and strong. She was the one you counted on when everything went wrong. As the last note of O'Carolan's tune slipped away into the evening, I started to put the fiddle down. I thought it might break my mother's heart.

But she said, "Charlie, please, don't

stop. Tears are my farewell to your pa. Just like your music is."

So I played another song. And then another. Little Polly fell fast asleep. She clutched her rag doll in one hand and Mama's skirt in the other. She held on tight to Mama like she was scared she would lose Mama too.

Music filled our house. It filled the space where Pa should have been. This was the farewell he would have wanted. I played for sorrow and I played for love. I played as well as I possibly could. Until I heard loud knocking at our door. And my bow hit a wrong note, sharp and sour.

Old Lady Grundy stood at the door, with Parson Bean behind her. She wouldn't come into our house. "I'll say what I have to say right here on the porch," she told my mama.

She said that she wouldn't be coming

to watch after Polly anymore. "It's just not safe," said Old Lady Grundy. "I've got my own family to think of."

"All right then, Mrs. Grundy," said my mother in a soft voice. "If that's what you feel you have to do. I suppose Charlie here can look after Polly while I go to school tomorrow. Just until I can find another sitter."

"Umm, er, yes, well..." Parson Bean spoke up. "You see, Mrs. Carroll, the school board doesn't think it is wise for you to come into school anymore. People are worried about their children. About the consumption, you see. You don't want to put those children at risk, if you've got the disease too, do you?"

"No, of course not," my mother said tightly.

When she closed the door and turned around, I saw that scared look on her face

again. That look that she had the night my pa died.

"Mama?" I said. I was embarrassed to hear my voice come out as high as Polly's. I was supposed to be the man of the family. But I sounded like a child.

"It's all right, Charlie," my mother said quickly. "It's all going to be all right."

But I looked at her face, all pinched and pale. And then I wondered if things would ever be all right in our family again.

CHAPTER TWO

A KNOCK ON THE DOOR

A month later we lost the house. My father had bought it just after he and Mama got married. It was a red brick house with stained-glass windows and a big porch covered with roses. I'd lived in that house all of my life. But we couldn't keep the payments up. So now we had to move.

We left town then, and went to live in the country with Pa's mother. She lived in

the Blue Ridge Mountains that divide North Carolina from Tennessee.

I had never met Granny Carroll. She never left her mountains. She was all the family we had left, because Mama had been an orphan and had no people of her own.

I knew that Pa had once worked hard to leave those very same mountains behind. He said he was proud to raise his own family in a town big enough for a college and a courthouse, where all the streets were paved. Old Lady Grundy had told me that Pa came from hillbilly folk. So I had asked Pa what hillbilly meant.

He said that's what city people call country people. He said we came from hardworking folk who had traveled all the way from Ireland. Ireland has the best fiddlers in the world, that's what my pa told me. Granny Carroll had carried Pa's

fiddle all the way from Dublin town. Pa said his people were honest farmers, and that I should never be ashamed.

But if he wasn't ashamed of his family, why had he worked so hard to leave them? He was running from something in those mountains, I reckoned. Sometimes he'd go back to visit with his mama in the years after Granddaddy Carroll died. But he never let us come along.

I think, in fact, that he *was* ashamed to have grown up in the mountains. My Granny's run-down, backwoods farm was as different from our house in town as night is different from day.

We went there in a hired horse-drawn cart. The journey took us several days. We had the entire state to cross, from the flatlands by the ocean in the east to the Blue Ridge Mountains in the west.

At first the mountains were nothing

more than a blue streak on the horizon. But then they grew, and grew, and grew. They grew until they filled the western sky. We passed through towns, each smaller than the last. And then there were only solitary farms with big white houses in tobacco fields. The houses grew farther and farther apart as the land turned wild around us.

When we reached the base of Black Mountain, the road became a narrow, rutted track. It snaked its way through a dense wood of oak and ash and thorn.

I didn't much like this lonesome place. I hated the bumpy, winding road. I missed our town's straight, level streets. And lamplight shining overhead.

The sun rode low upon the hills, casting shifting shadows. The wind moaned in the leaves above. Animals rustled in the undergrowth. A large hare darted across

our path. It startled the horses. I thought I heard a sound like laughter as our cart bumped to a halt.

The huge brown hare stopped and turned. Its fur was matted with brambles. Blood was encrusted on its long hind legs. It looked back at us boldly. Then it leapt into the shadows. I heard that sound, like laughter, again

I wanted very badly for that wagon to turn around and ride right back to town. Polly was clutching Mama's hand. Even Mama looked a little frightened. But I was supposed to be a man now. Not a child afraid of shadows. I took a deep breath. I straightened my back. And I reached for Polly's other hand.

"Let's sing 'She'll Be Comin' 'Round the Mountain,'" I suggested. I began the song. I raised my voice to be heard above the moaning wind.

We were still singing when the wagon pulled up to an old gray house in a clearing. When we saw our new home, our voices died. Mama's face was pinched again. That look was becoming permanent. It marked lines of age across her brow.

It wasn't a proper farm at all. Just a small house with a sagging front porch. The barn out back looked like it was going to collapse from sheer exhaustion.

Half a dozen scrawny chickens scratched in the bare dirt of the yard. Thin cows grazed in a pasture, and an old workhorse with a sway in his back stood swishing flies with his tail.

A tiny woman with hair of pure silver sat on the porch in a rocking chair. She was dressed in trousers and an old flannel shirt. In those days only men dressed that way.

The wagon driver unloaded our suit-cases and a trunk full of Pa's music. Then he tipped his cap and drove quickly away, muttering about the darkness coming on.

I stood and stared at the woman on the porch, not because of the clothes, but because her smile was just like my daddy's. Her skin was smooth as Irish cream and her eyes as blue as Polly's and mine. I thought at first she was too young to be our granny. But when she rose I could see her age in her stooped shoulders and shaking hands. She walked with the help of a carved wooden cane. She walked slowly, as though it were painful.

"Mary," Granny Carroll said, coming to embrace my mother. "It's good to see you again, lass."

Then she looked at me with one eye-brow cocked. It was an expression that I knew from my own mirror.

"You children are Carrolls, plain as the day," she said as she looked us over. Her voice still held a trace of the lilting accent she'd brought from the Irish hills. "You're going to be tall like your father, lad. You've got his strong hands as well. Those are fiddler's hands. Did he tell you that? Have you got that old Irish fiddle of his?"

"Yes, ma'am," I said. I kept it close. But I was still afraid to play it.

She smiled my daddy's smile again. "That's good," she said. "I've longed to hear music in this old house. There hasn't been any since your father left. I've gotten too old and stiff to hold a bow. That's why I passed my fiddle on to him."

I had heard the story of Granny Carroll carrying the fiddle all the way from Dublin town. But I had thought that my daddy learned to play from *his* daddy.

Maybe that was just because I did.

"So *you* were Pa's teacher?" I asked eagerly. I knew I still had a lot to learn. Maybe she could teach me.

"Me and the mountains, lad," Granny Carroll answered. She looked past me to the woods beyond.

I followed her gaze to the forest slopes. I shivered, but I didn't know why.

That night Granny Carroll asked to see Pa's fiddle. I took it from its battered old case. And I thought about Granny carrying it all the way across the Atlantic Ocean.

I put the fiddle in the old woman's hands. She stroked the wood with shaking fingers. Then she plucked the strings. The instrument was out of tune. She handed the fiddle back to me. "Tune her up, lad, and give us a song."

I tuned the fiddle warily. I didn't want to touch it, much less play it. I took a long time to rosin the bow while Granny watched me patiently. Finally I placed the fiddle beneath my chin. And then I began to play.

I meant to play a cheerful jig, an Irish tune, for Granny. But the sound that came from the fiddle's throat was a song of pain. It was sad and slow. Like the sound of a heart that was breaking in two. Or the sound of blood drawn from a stone.

"Stop it, Charlie!" my mother cried. There were tears in her eyes again. "Your Pa's fiddle is too out of tune. Play your own fiddle for us tonight. It has such a lovely sound."

Granny Carroll nodded. But I could tell that she knew I had tuned up Pa's fiddle just fine.

I got my own fiddle and started to play a reel called "Cat in the Hopper." Granny tapped the time with her cane. Her sharp eyes focused on the movement of my fingers. I finished the reel and I played two jigs: "The Pipe on the Hob" and "The Hag on the Churn." I knew my daddy would have been proud. My bow danced lightly over the strings, and Granny said, "He's got the gift."

Granny's eyes were bright with pleasure. They were drinking in the music like a thirsty man drinks water. Until I played "The Faery Reel." Then the pleasure drained from Granny's face.

"Not that song," the old woman said harshly. I lifted my bow from the fiddle strings. "Never play that tune inside this house! Not unless you want to wake the Good Neighbors. You'd best go and latch the door now, lad. Just in case they heard you play."

Although the nearest neighbor was miles down the road, I did as I was told. I barred the door. Then I looked at Mama with a question in my eyes. But my mother just sat there frowning.

"That's enough music for tonight," Granny said when I picked up my fiddle and bow again. She rose and pulled the parlor window shut. And then she shut the other windows as well. Even though the night was warm.

I put my fiddle away in its case. I knew I had done something wrong. But what? Granny Carroll was a stranger to me. She had rules and ways I didn't understand. I wondered if her old gray house would ever come to feel like home.

That night, I slept on the sofa, while Polly slept with Mama upstairs in Pa's old bed. I lay there missing my home, and the bedroom I'd had for all of my life. Granny's sofa was lumpy and hard. And the room felt stuffy and warm.

I rose to open the window again. A breeze was rattling the old glass panes. It seemed as if it were trying to find a way into the house.

When I lifted the window the night rushed in with the smells and the sounds of the forest. I heard an owl hooting somewhere in the trees. I heard the sharp bark of a fox. Even in town we had those sounds. But they seemed stranger, wilder here. The forest was alive at night. Creatures rustled in the undergrowth. Night birds cried in the dark. The wind was whispering through the trees, with a sound like voices I could almost understand. Yet I knew it couldn't really be voices because there were no other houses nearby. The wind was Granny's only neighbor. I opened the window wider, welcoming it into the house.

And that was my undoing. Granny did have neighbors, you see; neighbors the like of which I'd never dreamed. Disaster had come knocking on Granny's door. And like a perfect fool, I'd let it in.

CHAPTER THREE

THE MISCHIEVOUS GHOST

I tossed and turned the whole night through. My dreams were of dark nightmare woods. When morning came, I was glad to see the sun. For by dark the forest around Granny's house had seemed just as haunted as the landscape of my dreams.

The morning sun dissolved my fears. It turned the forest leaves to gold. The morning air was crisp and sweet, and mist was lifting from the highest hills.

Blackbirds perched upon the trees to serenade early risers.

But I wasn't the first one up, I discovered. Granny was in the kitchen already. Her hair hung down in a long silver braid as she stoked the fire in the stove.

She sent me out for firewood, and to pump water from the well out back. The well water had the strangest scent. It smelled like wildflowers and honey. I tasted it, and spat it out. It tasted foul, like moldy earth. Or fruit that had gone to rot.

I carried the bucket of water into the house and handed it to Granny. She took one sniff and dumped it out. She sent me down to the river instead, where the water would be fresh and clear.

A well-worn trail ran from the house and past the pasture to the river. As I started down the path, I noticed fresh tracks in the soft red clay. Animal tracks, and the tracks of horses' hooves. And footprints made by many passing feet—tiny feet, like a child's.

I filled the bucket and hurried back. I passed the paddock where Granny's old mare grazed. I stared at it as I went by. Someone had plaited the white mare's mane into a mess of tangled knots. Red berries hung like bells from the ends. Brambles were braided through the tail.

From behind me came the sound of laughter. High-pitched, like a child's. I whirled around. There was no one there. A rabbit scampered across the yard. A squirrel leapt from the barn roof to a tree.

I stared at the squirrel. For just a moment, I thought I'd seen it grasp the branch and pull itself up with little human hands. And I was sure that it was a human face that stared back at me. It was shaped like mine, but covered with fur. I blinked. No, my eyes were playing tricks. It was only a squirrel, that's all.

Granny Carroll frowned at me when I reported what I'd seen. "Our Neighbors have paid us a visit, right enough," she said as she stirred our morning grits in a big black iron pot. "I don't mean the farmboys down the road, my lad. I mean the folk who live underneath these hills. Some of them are good and some of them are bad. Just like any other folk. It's the bad ones you best beware of. You must be careful as you walk these woods."

"*Underneath* the hill, Granny?" I said. I stared at her blankly. "You mean like faeries or something—"

"Ssshhh!" she said. She gripped my arm. "You don't want to speak of them by name. It calls them, you see. You called them once already when you played their song. It's not good to draw their attention, lad. We'll have to be very careful now. Or there's no end of mischief they can cause."

I looked at Granny carefully. I wondered if I believed her. I'd seen the tracks and the mare's elflocks. But perhaps these were some farmboy's pranks. Just a trick to fool my Granny.

Granny let go of me and turned back to the pot. She said, "Back in Ireland, my mother taught me always to be careful of the Neighbors. We had an auntie over by Wicklow way who had a terrible time with the Wee Folk. There was a *phouka* that lived in her hearth. That's a nasty kind of Wee Folk, a *phouka*. Wouldn't leave the poor woman alone. When she came here to America, she thought she was quit of the creature at last. Her ship set sail, and one day on deck, there she sees the *phouka* sunning himself. 'And it's a fine day for sailing,' he says to her. Followed her all the way to Cincinnati."

"Did the fae—did the Wee Folk all come here from Ireland?" I asked.

"Well, now, that's what your Granddaddy Carroll used to say. He said the immigrants brought them along, just like my poor old auntie. But the Cherokee people have been in these mountains longer than any Irishmen. And they've got tales of magic too. They say Black Mountain is haunted, lad. With little people who live under the hill, and beautiful, deadly maidens who take the shape of deer. You're not sure whether you believe me. I can tell. But humor an old woman and be careful when you wander in the wood."

"I'll be careful," I promised Granny Carroll. The truth was, the forest already frightened me. It was a wild, lonesome kind of place. It stretched for hundreds and hundreds of miles. I felt that we were lost in the middle of it. I wanted to be back at home in town.

"Let this be a lesson, then. We were lucky we had the doors and windows shut. No telling what harm our Neighbors might have done if they had found a way in last night."

I remembered the open window. I felt a sudden stab of guilt. "Where's Mama and Polly?" I asked Granny. I still wasn't sure I believed her tales. But I needed to know that they were safe. I didn't like letting them out of my sight. They might slip away when I wasn't looking. Like Billy and Jimmy and Pa had done.

"Your mama is upstairs getting dressed. Polly is still fast asleep, poor lass. The journey has tuckered her out."

I climbed the creaking stairs to Pa's old room. Mama was combing her long dark hair. Polly lay sleeping like a chick in a nest made out of pillows and patchwork quilts.

I pushed the red curls from Polly's eyes. She frowned in her sleep. But she didn't wake. It had been a long journey for a girl just three years old. She did indeed look tuckered out. Her little face was drawn and pale.

I looked down at her for a long, long time. Then I kissed her. And I left her there to sleep.

CHAPTER FOUR

UNDER THE HILL

In the days to come we didn't talk much about Polly.

Oh, we talked about the daily things: Was Polly hungry? Did Polly want to go for a walk? Or help milk the cow? Or pet the cat? The answer was always no, no, and no. My lively little sister didn't want to do much of anything at all anymore. She just wanted to sit by the kitchen stove. Even when the day was warm.

There was one thing we were careful not to talk about. As Polly grew paler and weaker by the day, we never said the word *tuberculosis*. It was as though our silence would keep the disease away. We wove a thick cloak out of love and protection, to hide her from Death himself.

It was easy to keep our fear silent. We were too busy doing all the things that kept the old farm running. Its weedy garden, its thin cows and chickens had barely supported one old woman. And now there was a whole family to feed. And plenty of work to be done.

I didn't have time to think about our old life back in town. I didn't even have time to think about my pa. I was too busy learning to shovel and hoe. To milk a cow. To birth a goat. It was only when I slept that fear and sorrow caught up with me. My dreams were haunted by ghosts in the wood and the music of Pa's fiddle.

Mama put Pa's fiddle away in his

trunk. And Granny never asked me to play it again. But I played my own fiddle every night. Even when the skin on my hands grew rough from work. I had promised Pa I would keep on playing. I would drown out his haunted music with my own. It was the only thing that made little Polly smile as she lay there growing weaker day by day.

Our lives had become a piece of cloth slowly unraveling, thread by thread. There was never enough food. Never enough wood. Never enough hands for all the work to be done. I gave up hoping I could go back to school. All I hoped for was to make it through each day.

It seemed like the mountain itself had turned against us. Half the seeds we planted wouldn't grow. The rabbits ate whatever did. The barn cat just ignored the mice. The scrawny chickens wouldn't lay. At night the wind rattled the house. It cracked the old glass windowpanes, even when the rest of the forest stood still, without a single breeze.

Granny blamed the folk beneath the hill. Mama said this was foolishness. She told Granny this was America, and not to fill our heads with old Irish superstitions.

I wanted to agree with Mama. And sometimes during the daylight I did. But at night I'd hear that laughter again. The murmur of voices in the wind.

Something was watching from out in the forest. Something tapped on the windowpanes. I kept the windows tightly shut. It wanted me to let it in. It seemed to want something from us. And we had nothing left to give.

Granny sprinkled salt on the windowsills and tucked mountain ash leaves underneath our pillows. She hung a pair of old iron scissors on a hook above the door. These were charms to keep the Wee Folk out. But whenever Mama cleaned and swept, the leaves and salt would disappear. And then Granny would come along and put them back down again.

Granny left milk out for the Wee Folk at night. She left it in a little bowl on the front porch steps. One night before she went to bed Mama brought the bowl back in again.

"No sense in wasting good milk on the cat when there is barely enough for us," she said.

Granny shook her head. "No good will come of this," she told my mother sternly.

The next morning I went outside and discovered that Granny's cows were gone. The barn door stood wide open, although I'd locked it the night before. I saw fresh tracks in the soft red dirt. The tracks went every which way into the woods. It looked as if Granny had a dozen cows to go missing and not just three.

I searched all day, up the hills and down. Through bogs of mud and fields of thorns. I turned back home when night began to fall. I was weary and defeated.

When I reached the old gray house at last, the cows stood in the barnyard. They were chewing lazily on their cuds, waiting patiently for dinner.

Their hides were filthy, scratched by thorns. Their legs were caked with thick red mud. Their tails were knotted with vines that dragged behind them in the dirt.

They'd appeared again as mysteriously as they'd disappeared that morning. While I'd been led on a wild goose chase. And was as filthy, scratched up, and tired as the cows.

After that, the only milk we got from those cows was sour and curdled. One afternoon Mama sent me down the road to buy some milk from Mr. Bauer. His farm was five miles down the mountain road. Or four miles by the forest path.

By day I could almost forget the fear of the wood I would have by evening. Now the leaves were bright overhead. Sunshine dappled the path with gold. The ground was carpeted with bluebells and pockets of white mountain laurel. I saw deer roam through the alder trees, a pale-colored doe and her leggy fawn. I stood quite still and watched them pass. They moved with a dancer's grace.

There was a peacefulness in the woods by day unlike anything I'd ever felt in town. It made me forget our troubles on the farm. It soothed me like sweet music.

I wished that I had my fiddle with me now, to catch that peacefulness inside a tune. I hummed "Sweet Mountain Thyme" as I walked. I remembered how Pa used to play it. Mama would sing along with him in a voice that was high and clear.

The Bauer farm was larger than Granny's. It was a little less run-down as well. But it had that same wild, lonesome look that all the farms up on Black Mountain had.

I found Mr. Bauer mucking out his stable with the help of two young blond-headed boys. I figured they were his sons. They looked like twins, and seeing them made me miss Billy and Jimmy with a bitter pang.

The boys were shy with me, a stranger. They rarely saw people come around this way. They didn't seem at all like the kind who would laugh outside an old woman's windows. Or set her only cows astray.

Farmer Bauer gave me the milk. But he wouldn't take any pay for it. Not when he heard we had a sick child back home.

"Nearly lost my own, not two years back," he said. "My eldest son. On the porch there." He nodded to a pale young man who sat motionless in a chair.

"Is he all right?" I asked the farmer.

"As right as he ever will be. He's *tetched*, you see. He's not right in the head. Not since the ones under the hill got him. When he come back to us, he was like that."

"You mean the fae—" I began. Then I remembered my grandmother's warning. Farmer Bauer didn't seem to know it though. He named them right away.

"Faeries. That's what your granny would call them. My own granny back in

Sweden used to call them *skogsra*. Wood trolls. Some folks can see them. Some folks can't. My Johnny, he was one of the ones that could. Used to follow them on moonlit nights, on that path that runs from the river up the hill. He said the faeries used to dance up there. Then one night he came back and he was just like that." He motioned to the pale young man. "I guess they didn't take kindly to being watched."

He put a heavy hand on my shoulder. "I hear tell that you are a fiddler, boy. So I warn you, you be careful. Sometimes they steal children away. And they like musicians best of all. Musicians and babies and pretty young girls."

"Why would they do that?" I asked. My heart was heavy with dread. I thought of Granny's missing cows. And I wondered what would go missing next.

The farmer shrugged. "No one rightly knows. Maybe just because it amuses them."

He sat down on a tree stump and put tobacco in his corncob pipe. "There was a young woman who lived up yonder that the hill folk took seven years ago. Name of Sally Davis, I recall. A pretty little thing. And newly wed. The hill folk took her. Put a changeling in her place—a creature that looked just like Sally. The creature sickened and died. And the poor husband thought it was his bride that he was burying.

"No one ever would have known any different. But the young lady was smart, you see. She knew that if she ate the faeries' food she would have to stay under the hill forever. So she refused to eat it. The faeries had to bring her milk and bread and cheese. They'd steal it from the farms here about. Everybody had something missing.

"After a while the faeries got tired of it. They sent the young woman home again. But Sally's husband had married somebody else by then. Since he thought she was dead and all. So poor Sally Davis went back under the hill. I reckon she's still there to this day."

Johnny had turned to watch us while his father told this story. But when the story ended, the life seemed to drain out of him. He sat there like an empty husk. Like a body with no one within. His handsome face was pale and thin. It reminded me of Polly's.

The afternoon was growing late by the time I left the Bauer farm. I was halfway home, on the woodland path, when dusk began to fall. Twilight filled the mountain hollows with a blue-gray mist as thick as soup. It was hard to see the path I walked. I stumbled over roots and stones. I clutched the jug of milk and tried to ignore the laughing in the wind.

I thought about the things that Mr. Bauer and Granny had told me. I thought about faery changelings. I thought about Polly's worn little face. And an idea began to form in my mind. An idea that should have horrified me. What if that wasn't my sister at all, but a changeling left in her place?

Yet how could I be horrified, when the only other choice was more horrible still? If Polly had been stolen by the faeries, I still might be able to save her life. But if Polly had consumption, then I knew she would surely die.

I began to run. I flew through the wood. I ran blindly through the mist-draped trees. I reached the house, leapt the porch stairs, and burst through the kitchen door.

"Ssssh," said Mama. "Your sister is asleep. I don't want to disturb her."

Polly slept wrapped in Granny's quilts in a chair close by the stove. I handed the milk to Mama and went to stand by the child's side.

I looked into my sister's face. It was thin and pale and wrinkled now. She looked like a little old woman. She barely resembled my sister at all. Why had we never noticed the change? She had changed more than illness could account for.

"Where's Granny?" I asked Mama urgently.

"In the barn," Mama replied.

I went out to the barn. There was Granny. She was tying ropes around the necks of the cows. Stones with holes in the center hung from the ropes. *Hag stones* Granny called them. Protection against the faeries. There was salt sprinkled on the doorway. And an iron horseshoe nailed to the door.

"Granny, tell me about changelings," I said.

Granny looked at me sharply. Then she turned away. "Your Mama made me promise I wouldn't talk about Them in front of you or your sister anymore. And maybe she's right. She was born in this country. Maybe I'm too set in my old Irish ways."

"If you really believed that, you wouldn't be protecting the cows with salt and iron," I said. "Isn't Polly worth protecting too?"

She looked at me sadly. Then she shook her head. "A promise is a promise," she said sternly.

I kicked the cows' feed trough in frustration. I walked angrily back to the barn door.

"Charlie," she called. I stopped in the doorway. "You've been neglecting your fiddle, lad."

I gritted my teeth. How could she expect me to care about a fiddle now?

Was a fiddle worth more than flesh and blood? Even Pa hadn't thought so in the end.

"Charlie," she said. Her voice was hard. There was something desperate in it. "Your daddy had a trunk of sheet music. I think you'd best go practice."

I stood confused, remembering Pa's trunk. I hadn't looked inside it since the day my daddy died. I sensed that Granny was trying to tell me something, without breaking her promise to my mother.

"You're right, Gran," I said at last. I

had decided to trust her. There was something in that trunk I needed to see.

And I, too, had a promise to keep. I had promised my pa to hang on to the music. And to take care of Mama and Polly. No matter what it cost.

CHAPTER FIVE

THE STOLEN CHILD

My daddy's trunk, like my daddy's fiddle, had traveled all the way from Ireland. Written across it, in faded black paint, were the words: CARROLL, GRAFTON STREET, DUBLIN. DESTINATION: UNITED STATES.

I snapped open the trunk's brass lock. I lifted the heavy lid. Inside was Pa's old fiddle in its case, and books, and sheet music. The books were old and water-stained. The paper was brown and brittle. One was *The Fairy Mythology*, by a man named Thomas Keightley. The other was *Folk Tales of Ireland* by Reverend F. Xavier Carroll

I picked up the book by Reverend Carroll. I wondered if we were kin to him. It was full of tales about the faery folk. I opened it in the middle and began to read.

There was a couple up Sligo way whose baby was taken by the faeries. A changeling was put in the child's place and the parents never knew their own was gone. The changeling cried day after day. It wasted away to skin and bones. One day a neighbor girl came in to look after it. The parents left, and no sooner had the door swung closed behind them than the baby piped up in an old man's voice, "Have they gone at last? Quick! Get me a drink, lass. There's a whiskey bottle in the cupboard!"

✢   ✢   ✢

The parents drove the imposter from the house by threatening to throw it on the fire. I thought about the wan little child downstairs. I could never throw a child on the fire—changeling or not. I couldn't do it.

The Sligo couple never got their own child back. Or if they did, the Reverend didn't say. I thumbed through the Reverend's book and read about other changelings: stolen babes, stolen brides, nursemaids stolen for a faery child. In all his tales of people stolen away by the folk under the hill, there were none in which the captive ever came home again.

I picked up the other book and read about faery creatures from all over the world: the trolls of Sweden. The *nis* of Norway. The *rusalki* of Russia. The *Kobolde* of Germany. I read about the fox-faeries of Japan and the magical *peri* of Persia. I wondered if Granddaddy Carroll was right that the faeries had all come to America on the same ships that brought immigrants here from so many different lands.

Or maybe there had always been Wee Folk here, like the Cherokee Indian legends said. Maybe every land had faeries. Maybe only the names they went by changed. Well, it didn't matter. Whatever they were, they had stolen little Polly. And somehow I was going to find a way to steal my sister back.

I closed the trunk. Taking the books and the fiddle with me, I went downstairs. My mother looked at me with red-rimmed eyes. I could see that she was trying not to cry.

"Polly is awake," my mother said. "She doesn't seem to be doing well at all.

She's always hungry. Yet she's grown so thin. Oh, Charlie, I wish your pa was here."

Then she rushed past me and up the stairs as the tears began to fall.

Granny had come back into the house.

She was sitting by the stove with Polly.

Polly sat there with the same vacant stare that I had seen on Johnny Bauer.

Granny said, "Play some music for your sister, lad. That always seems to please her. Play 'King Orfeo' for her. Did your daddy teach you that one?"

"King Orfeo." I looked at Granny sharply. It was a song about the faeries. "I know it," I said. I put Pa's fiddle down. I picked up my own. I tuned it and played.

I saw Polly's eyes shift in her slack white face as my bow slid over the fiddle strings. I didn't sing the words of the song aloud. But Polly knew them as well as I. It was a favorite song in our family, especially among the children.

A king has to the hunting gone.
He's left his lady all alone.
The king of Faerie with his dart
Has pierced the lady to the heart.
And after them the king has gone.
And when he's come to the Faery Stone
He's taken out his fiddle and bow
Although his heart is filled with woe,
Although his heart is filled with woe.

And first he played the notes of joy,
And then he played the notes of pain,
And then he played the Faery Reel
And he played it o'er and o'er again....

I got excited as I played. I'd forgotten about this story. After the king plays for the faery host, they ask him what he wants for his playing: gold, silver, jewels? He wants only to take his lady home. And they tell him: *Rise and take her hand, take your lady and go.*

At the end of the song I stared at Polly's face. I was startled by what I saw. Her eyes were narrowed into slits. Her little mouth was twisted in a sneer. Her face was cold and mocking. It looked older than the hills. Then the moment passed, and her face went slack. It was vacant of life once more.

I got up and walked to the window. I felt salt beneath my hand where it rested on the sill. The moon was full and bright that night, frosting the trees with silver.

I turned and saw Granny's eyes on me. In her hands was Pa's green sweater. "It's cold tonight, lad. You'd best put this on."

The night was warm and muggy. But I

took the sweater from her. It was inside out and I started to reverse it. She stopped me with a tight grip on my arm.

I remembered then that Reverend Carroll's book had said wearing clothing inside out was a protection against enchantment. I put the sweater on the way it was. Inside the pockets was something grainy. I knew it was salt.

Granny said, "Take the child up to her bed for me, lad. I'm going to go see to your mama." She paused and looked at me carefully. "It's a fine night out there. But if you go out strolling, you'll be careful, my Charlie, won't you?"

"I'll be careful, Granny Carroll," I promised her.

She turned and hugged me tightly. Then stepped back, smoothing Pa's sweater around my shoulders. "Yes, you're going to be as tall as your father.

And as fine a fiddler. And as brave a man."

She took her cane. She slowly climbed the stairs. I followed after, carrying Polly—or whatever it was that had taken Polly's place.

The girl was light as feathers in my arms. She had wasted away to skin and bones. She looked up at me with cold, unblinking eyes. And the expression in those eyes was hatred.

CHAPTER SIX

THE HAUNTED MOUNTAIN

I put Polly into bed. Granny went down the hall to the other bedroom, where Mama was crying. I listened to the tap of Granny's cane, her slow footsteps, the door swinging shut.

I closed Polly's door and went down the stairs. I knew that if Granny had been any younger she would have been the one standing here. She would have been the one planning to go out into the woods.

And she would have known just where to go, and just what to do when she got there.

Instead it was only me, Charlie Carroll. City-bred and twelve years old. Scared of the woods, scared of the night. Scared of sickness, death, and ghosts.

Granny was wrong. I wasn't brave. I wasn't like my daddy. I wished Pa were with me now, saying, "You can do it, Charlie-boy." Like he always used to say to me whenever the tune was hard.

I put my fiddle in an old leather pack. Then I put Pa's fiddle in as well. A haunted fiddle for a haunted mountain. One for the notes of joy. And one for the notes of pain. Then I slipped quietly through the doorway and out into the light of the moon.

It was warm outside. But I kept Pa's sweater on. It still smelled of his pipe smoke. If I closed my eyes, I could imagine he was there.

Brambles clutched the sweater as I passed. Burrs and thistles clung to the green wool. I followed the path to the river, where Johnny Bauer used to wander at night and where I'd seen the prints of faery feet. I crossed the river on stepping-stones. And I took the path on the other side.

Here the trail led upward through the trees. It climbed the steep mountain slope. Moonlight altered the tall mountain oaks. They seemed alive. They stared down at me like giants with knotty branches for arms and twisted roots for feet.

I felt eyes watching as I passed. There was rustling in the underbrush. The wind was whistling through the wood. It sounded like a tune my pa used to play called "The False Knight on the Road."

I'd never climbed this path before. It took me up into unknown land. Oak and ash crowded the hill, thick with ivy and mistletoe. The path led to a steep stairway made of stones buried in ferns and moss. I settled my pack firmly on my back. I used both hands and feet to climb.

The stairs seemed to go on up forever. I felt as though I was climbing straight to the stars. My legs ached. But I climbed and climbed until at last I reached the top.

Here the land grew level again. The path led deep into the woods. The forest here was different from the forest down below. Here the trees grew straight and tall on slim white trunks turned to silver by the moon. A low mist swirled among the roots, stirred into motion by the wind. The song of the crickets was loud up here—an eerie tune, mournful and slow.

They sang a song of loneliness. Of love lost and dreams undone.

Suddenly, my path was crossed by a big brown hare. Its eyes gleamed red. I remembered the hare I'd seen before. The one who had looked at me just so boldly. The hare twitched its ears and showed its teeth. They seemed remarkably long and sharp. It lunged at me and I gave a cry. And then just as suddenly it was gone. I heard that whispery laughter in the wind. I took a deep breath and walked on.

Soon the sound of the crickets was joined by the sound of water in the distance. The path led to another river crossing, where dark water splashed over flat black stones.

I took off my shoes and waded across. Slimy moss was underfoot. When I left the river my feet were dark with something thicker than water.

I wiped my feet in the tall river grass. I felt sick to my stomach. When I'd cleaned every trace of blood from my toes, I laced my shoes back on again. The path left that dreadful river behind. I was glad. Even the sound it now made was frightening. It wasn't the gentle music of water. It was the low, moaning sound of something in pain. I didn't want to think about where an entire river of blood might have come from.

The path brought me out of the silver trees to a clearing. It was thick with briars. Cobwebs stretched across the trail. They glittered in the moon's soft light. I broke the cobwebs as I passed. I shuddered at their ghostly touch. A spider skittered across my cheek. I quickly brushed it away.

Briars reached out arms to snag me. I ripped away their knife-sharp claws.

Within the tangled briars I could see the shapes of old, bleached bones. A jawbone here. A rib cage there. From animals of every shape and size. Then I spied a human skull. And another. And a pile of human bones. Some of them were little. The bones of children, tangled in the briars. As though they'd been trapped in those vines and left to die and rot.

I looked away and took a deep breath. I continued on the mountain path. Ahead, two eyes looked back at me. They were round and soft and black as night. The golden doe stepped on my path. A fawn followed close behind. The doe leapt gracefully over the briars. As she leapt, I saw her change. I saw a woman with long black hair and a buckskin dress with beads and fringe. A young girl followed after her. She was as beautiful as the moon.

I felt a yearning deep inside me to leave the path and follow them. I took a step. I took another. I heard bones crunching underfoot. I thought about those human bones. Children trapped by strangling vines. I thought about Polly. And Mama back home. And Granny waiting, counting on me.

I forced myself back on the path. The deer maidens called out to me. They spoke in a language I did not understand. Perhaps they were speaking Cherokee. They sang a song so haunting that I longed to learn those words, that tune. My heart ached to follow them.

I put my hands over my ears. I could not turn my eyes away. But I would not leave the mountain path. The older deer maiden smiled at me. A beautiful smile, but cold. And cruel. Then she changed into a doe once more. She gave a kick and leapt over the trail. She headed back into the woods.

The younger maiden lingered a moment more. She also smiled before she changed. But her smile was sweet. It pierced my heart, and I almost left the trail. But the young deer maiden shook her head. Then she melted back into a fawn. And bounded away after the doe.

They seemed to take the night's beauty with them. Suddenly the forest was dark and cold. The moon disappeared behind black hills. The mist hid the pathway as I walked. An owl flew so close overhead I could feel the brush of its feathers as it passed. The bird was pure white. It looked at me with a tiny, wrinkled human face.

The trail looped back to the riverbank. I didn't want to return to it. But I remembered what Reverend Carroll wrote: *You must cross over running water three times to enter into faerieland.*

Here, at least, I would not have to wade again through that horrible river of blood. The river was crossed by an old stone bridge. Part of the bridge had tumbled away, damming up the river below.

At the side of the bridge sat a figure carved in stone. It was a little man with an owl's body. He had a stone cup clutched in his clawed feet. Someone had left three pennies in it, a feather, and a wedding ring.

I didn't have any coins to put in the cup in payment for my passage. I dug deep in my pockets. They were empty but for salt and lint. So I pulled a copper button off Pa's sweater. It came away with a bright piece of Mama's thread. I left it in the owl-man's cup. It glittered like fool's gold at the bottom.

When I crossed the bridge, the laughter stopped. I had grown used to the whisper of laughter following me. It was only when it stopped that I realized how constant it had been.

The wood was strangely silent now. Not a leaf stirred. Not an animal moved. My footsteps made no sound on the soft moss below my feet.

And then I heard it. The sound of a fiddle. Ever so faint. But unmistakable. The trail turned a corner and divided in two. One path was broad and clearly marked. One was narrow and overgrown. But there was no path to the place in the distance where the fiddle music came from. It was off in the forest to my left. In the darkest part of the wood.

I knew that sound. I trusted the music. For the first time in that long, long night I left the forest path.

The lines of an old song ran through my head:

The first road leads to wickedness.
The second road to righteousness.
The third road leads to fair Elfland, where
thou and I must go…

CHAPTER SEVEN

FINGERS LIKE TWIGS

I was half-blind in the dark of the woods. My shoes sank into moss and mud. Slippery things squelched underfoot. I dared not look. I pushed on through the trees and tangled undergrowth. I trusted my ears and the ribbon of music to lead me straight and true.

Even without my need to find my sister, I would have followed where that music led. It echoed through my very bones. It was the most beautiful sound I had ever heard. As though all the voices of wind, water, and earth had been woven into one song.

I had to see this fiddle player. I had to watch his fingers move. And then I understood my father. My father, who had loved music more than anything on this green earth.

At that moment I wasn't thinking about Polly. I was emptied of fear, and hope, and grief. There was nothing inside me but the beauty of that music. It was all that mattered to me.

Ahead the trees opened into a large clearing. A circle of long, silvery grass shimmered under a canopy of stars. Big stones marked the circle's edge. Some stood upright. Some had tumbled over. The mountains rose behind them, black against a moonlit sky.

And there was the fiddle player himself. He stood at the center of the circle. A tall, thin man with long, white hands and white hair fine as silken threads. I drew back into the shadow of the woods. The fiddler hadn't seen me. I hunched into the fork of a tree. And I listened to the fiddler play.

I heard only him, I saw only him, as I watched his fingers dance over the strings. His bow was as quick as a deer in flight and as graceful as a wood dove's wing. His fiddle was the color of moonlight. His clothes were black as the midnight sky. The music wove threads of color around him. The colors lingered when the song he played was done. They made lovely patterns in the light of the moon. Then slowly they faded away.

It was only then, when the music stopped, that I saw that there were others in the clearing. A moment before I would have sworn that the fiddle player and I were the only ones out upon the mountainside. Now the clearing was suddenly crowded. I crouched even farther into the shadows. I was frightened that someone would see me.

The faery host was spread across the hill. They perched on the old standing stones. They sprawled out in the silver grass. Smaller faeries whizzed overhead. Their wings flashed like fireflies. The faeries were laughing, feasting, fighting, stamping their feet and calling, "More! More!"

The faery fiddler obliged them. He quickly gave them another tune. I recognized the tune at once. It was a feasting song called "John Barleycorn."

The dancers spun around the ring. Their dancing was wild and astonishing.

Their feet stamped the earth. Their hands reached to the stars as they gave themselves music and delight.

My heart pounded as I looked for Polly. And there she was, at the edge of the ring. She sat cross-legged at a faery woman's feet. A silver cord was bound around her wrist. She looked like a pet upon a leash.

Her dress was dirty. Her feet were bare and filthy. Her hair was knotted up with vines and leaves. But she sat up tall. She was only three years old. But already I could see Mama's courage in her face.

The faery who had claimed her was a tall, skinny thing. I had heard the faeries called the Wee Folk so often that I thought they would all be smaller than me. But they came in many different shapes and sizes. Some were horribly, horribly ugly. With fingers like twigs and legs like stumps or brittle sticks. With woodland fungus growing from their ears. With tusks. Or hairy pelts. Or snouts. Others were beautiful beyond belief. They looked like they were made of water, or smoke. They trailed ribbons and pearls of light behind them wherever they stepped.

There were boys with hair like twigs or clumps of leaves. There were tiny laughing girls with brightly colored wings. There was one creature shaped like a porcupine with long human hands and huge flat feet. There was a man with a beak instead of a nose and mouth. And a woman with a fox's red tail.

Some, like the fiddler, seemed almost human. They were tall and slender. Their clothing shimmered the color of a mountain twilight. Their eyes were the gray of the morning mist. Their long, long hair was white as milk. Or black as the blackest midnight sky. They braided it up with ivy vines and dusted it with clouds of thistle seeds.

Something nipped my ankles. Hard. I cried aloud and turned to see a brown hare running off through the grass. And then another. And another. A dozen brown hares were leaping past my feet. I heard their familiar whispery laughter burst into the clearing.

They rolled in the grass. And as they rolled they changed from hares into brown-haired girls. Girls with rabbit ears and soft brown fur. One girl took me by the wrist. Her fingers were strong. Her teeth looked sharp. She pulled me into the clearing. The fiddle player stopped his song.

"Human boy, human boy," I heard the rabbit maidens call. The other faeries took up the chant. "Human boy, human boy..."

I was pulled into the stone circle. I looked over at Polly. She still sat at the edge of the crowd. She stared at me as though I was a ghost. Her hands were pressed across her mouth. I wondered if she dared not speak.

The faeries touched my hair and my cheek. They lifted my shirt and sniffed beneath. They took my pack and opened it. And they cried with great delight.

"A musician!" a crow-footed creature said.

"A musician!" was repeated through the crowd.

"A musician," the fiddler said with narrowed eyes. He frowned at me and looked me up and down. "I do challenge you then to play."

"A challenge!" The word was carried

around the circle. The faeries gathered close. Their eyes glittered.

"A challenge," I agreed. But I had no idea what I had just agreed to.

I took my fiddle from its case. I tightened the bow and tuned the strings. The crowd waited expectantly. All the faeries stared at me.

"Play," a rabbit girl whispered. She crouched like a hare beside my feet. "He has to match you. Then you match him."

This was a contest, I realized. I wondered what prize we were playing for. And what would happen if I lost.

I played the first tune I thought of. A reel called "The Hares on the Mountain." The fiddler matched me note for note. He played faster and faster, speeding up the pace. Then he changed the tune to another Irish reel. I recognized it. It was called "The Banshee."

I played along. I was shocked at how clumsy my best playing sounded next to his. I heard myself fumble the fingering. I missed several notes. And then a whole bar. But I kept on going. The fiddler and I continued to trade tunes back and forth: a reel, a slide, a waltz, and a jig. The faeries applauded their fiddler's nimble skill. And they roared with laughter over mine.

Yet I knew my father had taught me well. These were all tunes I had heard before. They were brought here from the Irish hills. I had heard them, played them, all of my life. I closed my eyes. I could almost imagine it was my father I was playing with still.

Then I opened my eyes. The fiddler had begun to play a song I didn't know. It sounded half-familiar, but I couldn't quite remember it. I followed along as best I could. I was missing the notes. Playing the wrong ones. The faery fiddler grinned wickedly. I knew he thought he had bested me. And I didn't know what would happen to me, or Polly, if I lost the challenge.

I thought hard and furiously. I struggled to keep up as he played. And then I knew why I partly recognized the tune. It was similar to one my daddy used to play. But his was not an Irish tune. It was a homegrown American one by the name of "Cripple Creek."

So I played the song the way I knew it best. The Southern country way that I'd been taught. The faeries' laughter quieted. The rabbit girl tugged at my sleeve, but I ignored her. I kept on playing. I played right over the faery fiddler's tune. I played louder and faster. And faster still. My bow flew over the strings. And then there was only the sound of my fiddle. The other fiddler had stopped playing.

He was listening to the tune with great delight. His white face wore a look of pure astonishment. Then he lifted his bow and he picked up the tune. He played along perfectly. Note for note. Yet I knew that I had won this contest. Or at least I had not lost it. We played "Cripple Creek" together, and the faeries began to cheer.

"A toast! A toast!" the faeries cried. "Bring food and wine for the human boy!"

When I finished the song, the faeries swarmed around me. Platters piled with strange fruits were lifted high. A wine cask was pressed up to my lips. I was powerfully thirsty. It all smelled wonderful.

"*No!*" came an urgent cry.

It was my sister Polly's voice. And it brought me to my senses. I recalled with a chill Farmer Bauer's tale of Sally Davis, who had saved herself only by refusing faery food and drink.

The faeries backed away from me. The faery woman petted Polly's head, as though my sister were a dog or a cat.

"What's the matter, my pet?" she said to Polly. "Don't you want a companion under the hill?" Her voice was low and musical, with something like my Granny's lilt.

"I haven't come to follow you under the hill," I told the faery host. "I've come to fetch my sister home again."

"Impossible!" the fox-tailed woman cried.

"Why should we let her go?" said a twig boy.

"No, you must stay and play for our

dance," said the rabbit maidens crouched around my feet.

"I'll make a deal with you," I said. I knew faeries could not resist a bargain. "I'll play for your dance, right here, tonight. But then you have to let us go. And promise us you'll do no harm to our family. Or to our farm."

The faery fiddler smiled slyly. "I believe I shall accept your bargain, sir. But we intend to dance until dawn. You must play until the sun comes up. If you stop, even once, the child is ours. And you shall be ours as well."

I agreed, for what choice did I have? And dawn could not be that far off. I'd been climbing through the woods for hours. Surely the sun would rise soon.

I fear I did not realize that time passes strangely among the faery folk. In fact, dawn was still many hours away.

I was tired and footsore. My fingers were already stiff. But I took my pack and I took my fiddle and went to stand in the center of the clearing. The dancers made a circle around me.

And I began to play.

CHAPTER EIGHT

THE LONGEST NIGHT

I played and I played. One song after another. I played every song I had ever heard. American tunes and Irish tunes. And tunes that I made up right on the spot.

The faeries never seemed to tire. Overhead, the moon never seemed to move. The night went on, and I kept on playing. The faery fiddler kept right along. He learned these tunes as fast as I could play them. His fingers flew, twice as nimble as mine.

Every time I tired, every time I slowed, the faeries would laugh and the fiddler would grin. Then I'd look at Polly's brave little face and I'd pick up the rhythm again.

The faeries danced like strange, mad creatures, their heads flung back, spinning fast and wild. It made me dizzy to watch them dance. I looked up at the stars instead. I prayed for the sun to rise.

The hours crept by. My hands were sore. My fingertips were raw and painful. But the music itself seemed to lift me whenever my strength began to falter. I played on fiercely, scowling, in a white heat of determination. I could almost hear my daddy's voice in my ear saying, "You can do it, Charlie-boy."

At last the moon sat low on the hills. It

rode the backs of the mountains. A thin line of blue sky separated the black night from the black mountain tops. Dawn was somewhere behind those hills. I prayed it would come in time.

The faery fiddler saw this too. He frowned. His gray eyes narrowed. I could see the stubborn set of his face. He was not going to lose another challenge.

"The dawn!" the crow-footed creature cried. "It's coming! The dawn! It's coming!"

"He'll win," hissed the woman with the red foxtail.

"Never!" cried the other faeries.

The faery woman who stood with Polly pointed a long white finger at me.

The bow in my hand became red hot. "You're cheating!" I cried.

The woman laughed. The bow grew even hotter.

I continued to play. It's just a trick, I told myself. *It's just magic. It isn't really happening.* If it were real, my hand would have blistered and burned. But it *felt* real. My hand was in agony. Yet I held on tight and kept on playing. I bit my lip against the pain.

Then the bow began to hiss. It was a snake's tail I held. The snake barred its fangs close to my face and flicked out a long, forked tongue. I squeezed my eyes shut and held on tight. I played even louder and faster.

Then the fiddle in my hand become a flaming branch. The fire licked upward at me. Smoke stung my eyes and made me cough. I moved my bow through the smoke and the flames. I missed a note, and then another. But still I played on.

The faces around me were growing angry. The dancers no longer danced with delight. Their dance looked menacing to me. I gritted my teeth and began another reel. I tried to hold on until the dawn.

I remembered Pa's last words to me: *Don't let go of the music, boy.* I wouldn't let go. I clutched the fiddle tight. I gave the music everything I had to give.

The crowd surged around me, the dancers, the watchers. Polly was pulled forward along with the rest. She was close to me now—almost at my feet. If only I could just snatch her and run.

The twig boys jostled me. A flying faery pulled my hair. A bat-winged creature chewed my ear. The rabbit maidens nipped my feet. But I wasn't going to let the crowd rattle me. And so I kept on playing.

A faery landed on my head. It sat there, pounding out the rhythm of the music with its tiny fists. I tossed my head and it held on tight. But still I kept on playing.

A huge creature with a hairy pelt stepped close. The creature stank. I stepped away. I played a polka, as sprightly as I could make it. The tune made the rabbit maidens laugh. They clapped their hands. They slapped my back. They pulled the huge creature away to join the dance.

Overhead the sky was beginning to lighten. The owl with an old man's face flew above. It hissed at me, low and menacing. It snatched my fiddle right from my grasp.

I stood dumbfounded. And empty-handed.

"Charlie! Here!" little Polly cried. She had taken Pa's fiddle out of my pack. She threw it up to me with a three-year-old's aim. I had to lunge to grab it by its neck.

I played it as I tuned it—a horrible sound. It made the faeries shriek. They clapped their hands over their ears. Then I played a song called "The Faery's Lament."

They stepped back. And they let me play.

The voice of the fiddle was low and deep. Yet it carried across the grassy plain. It carried the sound of my father's grief. Of his love for the two sons he had lost, and the dreams that had died along with them.

The faery host sank to the ground with the weight of my father's sorrow.

Tears rolled down those pale white cheeks. Just as tears rolled down my own.

I played as the sky grew pearly gray and the mist rose from the mountain tops. The faery fiddler did not play along. He sat on the ground, his proud head bowed. And he cried for my father's loss.

Yet as I played I heard the song change. Slowly it became higher. And sweeter. I played through to the end of Pa's sorrow. And I came to the music my Pa would have found, if only Death had not found him first.

It was a lilting air. It was a tune made of love, not just for the twins, but for life itself. For the breath in our lungs and the good earth underfoot. And for the sun rising early on the mountains.

I was still playing as the sun cleared the hills. I was playing a tune called "The Morning Dew." I was playing all alone, a soft gentle sound, for the faery fiddler had gone.

The faery host were fading with the sun, like the mist rising from the distant hills. And then there was only Polly and me. As though the faeries had never been there at all. Only the grass of the clearing showed that I hadn't dreamed that contest. The grass was trampled in a perfect ring, sparkling in the morning light.

I put Pa's fiddle down and reached for my sister. We clung to each other on the bare hillside. She smelled like the faeries, of wildflowers and honey. But her cheeks were healthy and rosy and plump.

I picked her up and I picked up Pa's fiddle. I turned toward the path that would lead us down the hill.

My own fiddle was lost to the faeries, but I no longer had any fear of Pa's. It had changed that night. The old Irish fiddle was now the color of moonlight. And it played sweeter than any fiddle I had ever heard.

CHAPTER NINE

WHEN THE MOON IS RIGHT

As we walked wearily back to the farm, I wondered what I was going to tell Mama. Granny would understand everything. But what was my mama going to say when she saw that there were two Pollys—our own, and that pale, sickly creature in Polly's bed?

And what would we do with the changeling now that we had our own Polly back again? I wasn't going to threaten the poor thing with the fire, no matter what the Reverend Carroll's book had said. Perhaps we'd just have to keep her. Fatten her up with loving and Granny's cooking.

The house was quiet as we approached. It was still early; I thought Mama would be asleep. But she was up, along with Granny Carroll. They were waiting on the front porch steps.

Mama cried aloud when she saw us come. She held us tight and then took Polly from my arms. She kissed my sister over and over, while my Granny looked on with a great smile.

Granny took me inside. She made me sit down, and cooked me what she called a Hero's Breakfast. And then she told me the story of what had happened while I was gone.

Early in the morning they'd heard

curses, and banging on the door. Mama and Granny had gone downstairs together. Mama held Granny's cane like a club. But when she opened the door there was only a strange little woman standing there.

The little woman was pale and thin. She was dressed in leaves and rags, and wore a red cap on her head.

She cried, "I want my own child back, now that your son has come claimed yours!"

And at that, the little changeling appeared. She ran swiftly down the stairs. She no longer looked like Polly at all. She had fingers like twigs and leaves for hair.

"Mama, Mama," the creature cried. She jumped into the stranger's arms. And off they went, as quick as you please, while Mama just watched in shock.

After that, my Mama was willing to sit

and listen to Granny Carroll's advice. And that's how they came to be sitting on the porch that morning, waiting for us to come home.

It's just as well that my mother decided she'd better believe in faeries. There were a lot of them around the place after that. And they were true to their word. They didn't cause mischief. In fact, they helped us with the work of the farm. They came at night, while we slept. We'd wake up and find our chores already done.

Before long we had the best garden for miles around. Our well water tasted wonderful—like wildflowers and honey. We had a whole herd of dairy cows, their milk as thick as the finest cream. And I even got to go back to school, in the schoolhouse at the bottom of Black Mountain.

I always kept my promise to my pa. I grew up to be a fiddle man. Folks say there's no better fiddle player between here and Dublin town.

But I know there's one. The faery fiddler. I'll never be as good. Not if I live a hundred years

And so, on moonlit nights I still go wandering in the forest. Even though I'm an old man now and it's not so easy to find my way. On certain nights, when the moon is right, I can hear the whisper of laughter in the air.

And then, if I listen carefully, I can hear that fiddler play.

Terri Windling has always loved old faery stories like the Irish "changeling" legends. She once lived in Ireland, but now lives in a small village in England during the summer and in the Arizona desert during the winter. She has two cats in one house, three cats in the other, and lots of faeries in both.

Ms. Windling has family in the Blue Ridge Mountains of North Carolina, in an area very much like the one in this story. Years ago, people from Ireland and other countries settled there, bringing all kinds of folk tales and folk music with them. All the melodies Charlie Carroll plays in this story are actual folk tunes that people play to this very day.

BULLSEYE CHILLERS™

Camp Zombie
Camp Zombie: The Second Summer
The Changeling
Dr. Jekyll and Mr. Hyde
Edgar Allan Poe's Tales of Terror
Fangs of Evil
Frankenstein
The Mummy Awakes
The Phantom of the Opera
Return of the Werewolf
Shadow of the Fox
The Vampire

Another Bullseye series you will enjoy:

BULLSEYE STEP INTO CLASSICS™

Anne of Green Gables
Black Beauty
Kidnapped
Knights of the Round Table
Les Miserables
A Little Princess
Little Women
Mysteries of Sherlock Holmes
Oliver Twist
Peter Pan
Robin Hood
The Secret Garden
The Three Musketeers
The Time Machine
Treasure Island
20,000 Leagues Under the Sea